Dear mouse friends,
Welcome to the world of

Geronimo Stilton

THE RODENT'S GAZETTE
EDITORIAL STAFF

Geronimo Stilton
A learned and brainy
mouse; editor of
The Rodent's Gazette

Thea Stilton
Geronimo's sister and
special correspondent at
The Rodent's Gazette

Trap Stilton
An awful joker;
Geronimo's cousin and
owner of the store
Cheap Junk for Less

Benjamin Stilton
A sweet and loving
nine-year-old mouse;
Geronimo's favorite
nephew

Geronimo Stilton

CYBER-THIEF SHOWDOWN

Scholastic Inc.

Published by Scholastic Inc., *Publishers since 1920,* 557 Broadway, New York, NY 10012. SCHOLASTIC and associated logos are trademarks and/or registered trademarks of Scholastic Inc.

ISBN 978-1-338-21519-9

Text by Geronimo Stilton
Original title *C'è un pirata in internet*
Cover by Giuseppe Ferrario
Illustrations by Giuseppe Ferrario (design), Roberta Bianchi (pencils), and Giulia Zaffaroni (color)
Graphics by Chiara Cebraro

Special thanks to Tracey West
Translated by Anna Pizzelli
Interior design by Becky James

10 9 8 7 6 5 4 3 2 1 18 19 20 21 22

Printed in the U.S.A. 40
First printing 2018

I Was One Happy Rodent!

My dear readers, it all started early one morning, when I woke up feeling as fresh as newly made mozzarella!

I felt very happy — as happy as a rat in a cheese factory!

Why was I in such a GREAT MOOD? Well, I woke up to warm, bright sunlight shining on my snout. The little birds were chirping. There was a whiff in the air of freshly baked CHEESE BREAD . . .

Yes, it was one of those days when you want to say to every rodent in the whole wide world: "Life is beautiful and the world is mousetastic!"

I was in such a good mood that I decided to work out (*which does not happen too often . . .*)!

Then I brushed my teeth. I took a quick shower, humming one of my favorite

tunes, and quickly got dressed to go to work.

And what is my **job**, you ask?

The most amazing job in the world!

I run *The Rodent's Gazette*, Mouse Island's most famouse newspaper.

My name is Stilton, *Geronimo Stilton*! And when I walked to the office that morning, I greeted everyone I saw with a smile.

First, I ran into Miss Angel Paws, Benjamin's teacher, on her way to school.

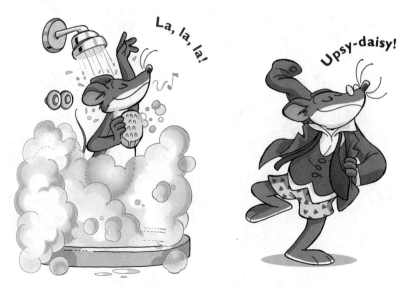

"**Good morning, Miss Paws!**" I squeaked, waving to her.

But she looked the other way. It didn't bother me. I just assumed that she hadn't heard me.

Then I ran into Samantha Squeaky Clean, my housecleaner.

I have known her for a long time. She is always kind, helpful, and friendly.

"**Good morning, Miss Squeaky Clean!**" I squeaked with a smile.

She looked at me and scowled. "Hmph!"

At the moment, it didn't bother me. I figured that she was in a bad mood.

Then I ran into my tailor, Sartorius Stitchfur.

"Hello," I said politely, but he didn't reply, either. Weird! Was he also in a **bad mood**?

Next, I said hello to Mrs. Busymouse. We have been **neighbors** for a long time. I help her with her grocery shopping, and every day I send her a **large-print** copy of *The Rodent's Gazette* because she is older and has trouble reading the small print.

But she frowned at me. "Shame on you, Geronimo," she said in a disapproving tone.

I wondered if maybe I forgot her birthday.

"Hmm . . . I am sorry," I replied. "Have a great day!"

Still looking **OUTRAGED**, she turned and walked away.

I started thinking that some **outbreak** of a weird bad mood was spreading in New Mouse City. Otherwise, why was everyone being so **unfriendly**?

The rest of my walk was exactly the same. I smiled at every rodent I passed, but nobody would greet me. Everyone turned the other way, pretending not to see me or replying in a **RUDE WAY**.

Pretty soon I started to wonder if the bad mood outbreak was contagious, because my happy mood turned more and more **rotten** with each step I took!

I only realized what was **wrong** after I reached the newsstand. All the newspapers (except for *The Rodent's Gazette*) featured

terrible stories about me on the front.

What was going on?

Red in the snout from **embarrassment**, I bought all the newspapers. Then I quickly walked to the office, **HIDING** behind the big **stack** so nobody could see me.

What bad manners!
What?
Grrrr!
Grunt!

You Should Be Ashamed of Yourself!

I called out, "Good morning!" when I walked into the office, but NOBODY replied.

Everyone turned the other way, looking insulted, or pretended not to hear me.

"Really? All of you have turned against me, too?" I cried.

I STOMPED into my office, SLAMMED the door behind me, and put the stack of newspapers on my desk. Each one had a terrible, awful, HORRIBLE story about me on the front page. I was making headline news — and the news wasn't good at all!

I looked over the PHOTOS and what I saw

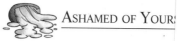

left me squeakless. In one of them, I was stepping on the mayor's paw! In another one, I was TRIPPING a mouselet who was dancing with me! In the next one, I sneezed right onto a helpless stranger . . .

HOW WAS THAT POSSIBLE? I am a well-behaved mouse who always tries to be kind to everyone. I had never done any of those things! But it was definitely me in those photos!

HOW WEIRD . . .

I started looking at them more carefully, and then it hit me. These were similar to photos that I had posted online after a party for the mayor.

I remembered the photos well, but someone had changed them. I had never stepped on the mayor's paw, nor tripped a mouselet, nor sneezed on someone! They had been EDITED!

WHO had done this to the photos and, more important, WHY? I wondered.

I was thinking about this when my grandfather, William Shortpaws, barged into my office. He slammed a copy of The Daily Rat on my desk.

"You should be **ashamed** of yourself, Geronimo! Is this any way to behave?" he scolded me.

Then my sister, Thea, walked in, with a draft of my latest **BOOK**, full of red marks.

"Ger, your latest book is full of mistakes!" she reported.

"Mistakes?" I asked.

"Yes!" Thea replied. "It's like you forgot

Help Geronimo Spot the Differences!

Photo taken by Thea

Edited photo

Photo taken by Thea

Edited photo

Photo taken by Thea

Edited photo

all about GRAMMAR, spelling, and PUNCTUATION!"

Then one of the assistant editors, Ms. Raven, walked in. "Geronimo, is this some kind of a joke?" she asked, waving a printout of an email. "Why would you send out these mean emails to the whole staff? This one says that we all had stinky cheese breath. That's not very nice!"

"What has gotten into you, grandson?" my grandfather boomed. "DO YOU HAVE CAT TREATS FOR BRAINS?"

"I — I —" I stammered. I didn't know what to say. I might as well have had cat treats for brains, because I was so confused that I couldn't think straight!

Nothing made any sense!

I knew that I hadn't sent Thea a book manuscript filled with mistakes. I read each draft a THOUSAND times to make sure grammar, spelling, and punctuation were correct.

And I certainly hadn't sent out an email to my staff telling them that they had cheese breath. I don't have a mean whisker in my body!

"I SWEAR, I didn't send those emails," I said.

Ms. Raven slapped a pile of papers on my desk.

"Read them yourself," she said, and then she walked out of my office.

I quickly read through the emails. They were CLEARLY sent from my email address. And each one was just as offensive and mean as the stinky cheese breath email.

One of them said, "You are more annoying than gum stuck in my fur!" Another said, "Your stories are so boring they put me to sleep!"

"**It's not possible!**" I said. "I would never send these kinds of emails to my coworkers. They're like my second **family**!"

Thea and Grandfather Stilton walked out, shaking their heads. I began to sob.

"**WHY, OH WHY, IS THIS HAPPENING TO ME?**"

THINGS GET WORSE!

Just as I stopped crying, a delivery mouse knocked on my door, and behind him there was **another one**, and **another one**, and **another one**. Each one was carrying a different *useless* yet terribly EXPENSIVE object in his paws.

The first had a pair of tap-dancing shoes

I didn't order anything!
THEY DELIVERED THE FOLLOWING:
TAP SHOES
A GOLD-PLATED SUITCASE

once owned by the famouse dancer, Fred Fancyfoot (*totally useless since I don't tap-dance!*). The second had a huge gold-plated suitcase (*totally useless because it was so heavy you needed a crane to lift it up!*). The third had keys to a private purple helicopter (*totally useless, as I do not have a license to fly a helicopter!*). The fourth had a guitar decorated with precious stones (*totally useless because I cannot play the guitar!*).

"**HOLEY CHEESE**, take these things back!" I shrieked. "I did not order them. I do not

need them. And most important, **I do not want them**!"

The first delivery mouse shrugged. "Sorry, sir, but you **ordered** all of this stuff from the **Filthy Rich Rats** website. It was all paid for using your credit card. It's not our **fault** you changed your mind!"

They deposited their deliveries and then walked out.

I scratched my **furry** head. Was it possible that I had purchased all of these objects?

Maybe my head was full of **cat treats** after all . . .

Before I could add up the cost of those EXPENSIVE items, more delivery mice came into my office! They had more ridiculous items for me. There was a **solid-gold statue** of me on a horse (*riding horses makes me nervous!*).

And the gifts kept coming. One mouse carried in a new armchair studded with

A COLLECTION OF ANCIENT CHEESE RINDS

KEYS TO A FURRARI

jewels (*totally useless, because I already had an armchair, and the precious stones were sharp!*). Another held a collection of ancient cheese rinds belonging to Mousehoptep III, stored in a real Egyptian vase (*a treasure fit for a museum!*).

Finally, a delivery mouse handed me the keys to a Furrari race car (*totally useless because I am afraid to drive fast cars!*).

Then the phone rang. **LEDGER MONEYPAWS**, the manager of the bank was calling me.

"Mr. Stilton, I am so sorry to have to tell you this, but your savings account is empty," he began. "**You are broke!**"

"Broke? What? How is that possible?" I squealed.

"It is **VERY POSSIBLE**,

Mr. Stilton, because you have spent every **penny** that you had — and more. You **OVERCHARGED** your credit card, and now you **OWE** the bank a great deal of money," he explained.

I couldn't believe my ears. "I what?"

"You owe us a lot of **MONEY**. Cash. Greenbacks. Bills," Mr. Moneypaws said. "I must say, Mr. Stilton, that I thought you were a very **sensible** mouse. What exactly do you need with a **golden statue** of yourself? And a **jewel-encrusted** armchair?"

"But I didn't **buy** those things, I swear!" I protested.

"Do not **LIE** to me, Mr. Stilton," Mr. Moneypaws said sternly. "These charges were clearly made from your very own **COMPUTER**. And now to pay your debt, I'm afraid you will have to sell *The*

Rodent's Gazette. I hate to think what your grandfather will say."

I started to beg. "My grandfather? Please don't say a **word** to my grandfather!"

Then I fainted, falling backward onto my office floor.

I'm not sure how long I was out. I just knew that I did not want to wake up. I was dreaming about a green-eyed mouselet who was scolding me.

"Bad, really bad, Stilton," she was saying.

"Did you already forget the **Golden Rules**?"

"I am sorry, miss, do I know you?" I asked.

Before she could answer, a bucketful of **COLD WATER** splashed on my snout and I woke up, *sputtering*.

I opened my eyes and saw my sister, Thea, standing above me, holding a bucket in

her paws. Next to her stood my dear little nephew Benjamin, who looked worried . . . very worried!

"Uncle Ger, are you okay?" he asked.

I slowly stood up and rubbed my eyes.

"I must have fainted," I replied. "I was dreaming about a mysterious mouselet with green eyes and RED FUR. I couldn't explain it, but I had the feeling she was the only one who could help me!"

Thea and Benjamin looked at each other in surprise. They squeaked at the same time: "But of course, we know exactly who you mean!"

"You do?" I asked.

Thea and Benjamin didn't answer me. They just grabbed me by my sleeves and

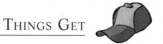

DRAGGED me out of my office . . .

"Where are we going?" I squeaked as they pulled me.

She's My Only Hope!

We hopped in Thea's car and she **TOOK OFF** toward the harbor.

"Hey, **SLOW DOWN**!" I squeaked. "Where are we rushing to?"

Thea grinned. "We are driving to see **someone**! The only one who can help you!"

"Can you please tell me who **SHE** is?" I pleaded. "You're talking about the mysterious rodent in my dream, right?"

"Come on, Uncle G, don't you remember who **SHE** is?" Benjamin asked.

"**CHEESE AND CRACKERS**, just please tell me!" I begged.

"She is Professor Margo Bitmouse, also known as Doc," my nephew replied.

NAME: MARGO BITMOUSE

NICKNAME: DOC

JOB: COMPUTER SCIENTIST

HOW GERONIMO KNOWS HER: SHE TAUGHT A CLASS IN INTERNET SAFETY AT THE INSTITUTE FOR MARINE M.O.U.S.E.O.L.O.G.Y. AND GERONIMO TOOK THE CLASS. SHE IS ALSO FRIENDS WITH HIS SISTER, THEA.

HER SPECIALTY: VIRTUAL REALITY VIDEO GAMES

HER HOBBY: WRITING CODE

HER DREAM: TO DEFEAT ALL HACKERS AND CYBER CRIMINALS

"Bitmouse?" I repeated.

Benjamin shook his head. "You totally forgot everything, Uncle G. That's why you are in such big trouble!"

By then we had arrived at New Mouse City Harbor. We stopped in front of a **building** that I recognized. A wooden sign hung over the door:

INSTITUTE FOR MARINE M.O.U.S.E.O.L.O.G.Y.

Finally, I remembered! A few years before, I had attended a class on **Internet safety** there. It was taught by Margo Bitmouse, the foremost **expert** on Internet safety in all of Mouse Island. She was the GREEN-EYED mouse in my dream.

Doc (as everyone calls her) teaches a **popular** Internet safety class geared toward technologically challenged, hopeless rodents . . . like me! But why were Thea and

Benjamin bringing me to her? I couldn't remember anything I learned in that class — maybe that was the problem!

Thea pulled up in front of a ship, the Scrolling Surfer. "Doc has set up a new onboard school," my sister explained.

Thea spotted Doc on the deck and called out to her. "Hello, Doc! We need your help. It's an EMERGENCY!"

"Come on board!" she called back with a smile. "We're about to ship out!"

We climbed onto the ship, Doc raised the anchor, and the *Scrolling Surfer* took off from the harbor, as fast and smooth as a seagull . . .

I was surprised to see my uncle Grayfur at the ship's wheel. I waved and then Doc asked us to FOLLOW her to the meeting room, where we sat around an oval glass table.

"Doc, I'm pleased to see you again," I said, shaking her paw.

"I am, too, Stilton," she firmly replied. "But something tells me you probably forgot everything that I taught you, especially the ten Golden Rules! Right? Otherwise you would not be in trouble."

I blushed to the tips of my ears. She was right! But I didn't want to admit it.

"Hmm . . . well . . ." I mumbled. "It's not that I completely forgot. I mean, I guess I forgot a little bit . . ."

She arched her eyebrows and stared at me with her GREEN eyes. I couldn't lie.

"All right, I admit it," I said. "I forgot everything, especially the ten Golden Rules! But, Doc, what do the rules have to do with what happened to me?"

"That's what we're about to find out,

Ha, ha!
Look!

Le dieci Regole d'Oro
1) Occhio alle secche
7) Ci incontriamo? No, grazie!
9) Alla larga dai maleducati!
10) Occhio al portafoglio!
1
7
8
6

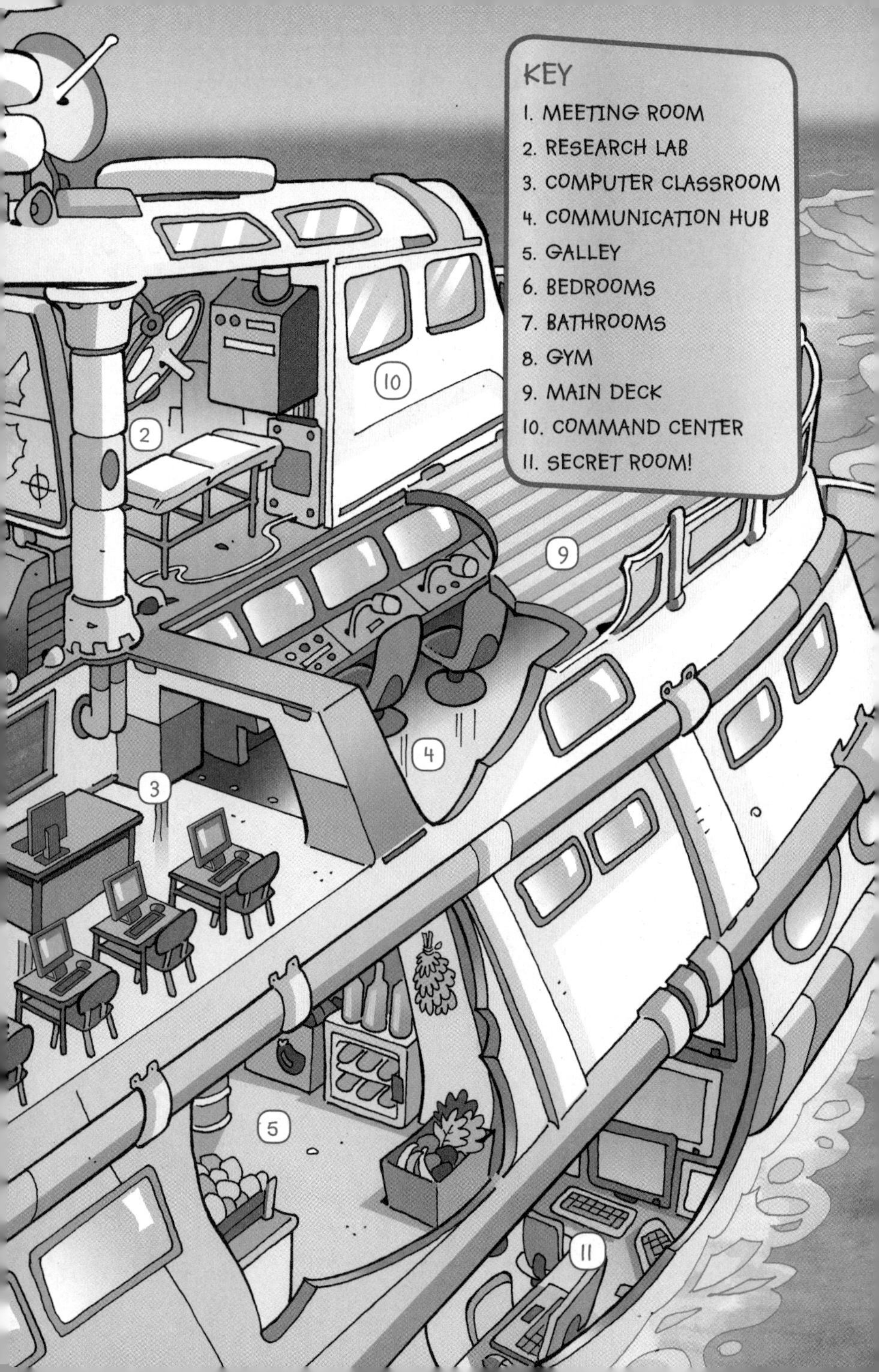
KEY
1. MEETING ROOM
2. RESEARCH LAB
3. COMPUTER CLASSROOM
4. COMMUNICATION HUB
5. GALLEY
6. BEDROOMS
7. BATHROOMS
8. GYM
9. MAIN DECK
10. COMMAND CENTER
11. SECRET ROOM!
10
2
9
4
3
5
11

Stilton," she replied. Then she pointed to a picture with a golden frame hanging on the wall. It was a list of the ten **Golden Rules** of Internet safety.

"Study them, Stilton," she ordered, "and then I will quiz you!"

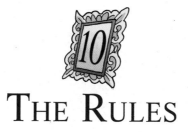

10

The Rules

I got closer to the picture and read the ten Golden Rules, while my ears became REDDER AND REDDER with embarrassment.

It was true. I had totally forgotten everything. How could I not remember all of this important stuff!

"Doc, I reviewed the rules," I said, walking back to the table. "Can you HELP me figure out what's happening?"

"I told you I would quiz you, Stilton," she said. "If you can recite all ten rules, I will help you."

I took a deep breath. I was so anxious that my whiskers were trembling. Then I perfectly recited the ten Golden Rules . . .

10

The Ten Golden Rules

1. Always surf the web with the help of an adult!
2. Make sure your laptop has a strong password!
3. Never click on suspicious links!
4. Do not mail photos and personal information to people you do not know!
5. Tell your parents if you receive personal pictures from people you do not know!
6. If someone sends you a message that makes you feel uncomfortable, tell an adult.
7. If a stranger asks to meet with you, tell your parents!
8. Some websites might ask for money — stay away from them!
9. Use common sense when surfing the web!
10. Do not post anything online that is hurtful to other people.

"Very good, Stilton," Doc said with a nod. "Now what can I do for you? What is the EMERGENCY your sister, Thea, was talking about?"

Thea answered for me. "Doc, I think someone HACKED into all of my brother's online accounts. He's really gotten himself into trouble!" she said.

I sighed. "Thea is right. Someone accessed my computer while I was online, copied my PHOTOS, edited them to make me look like I was behaving in RUDE WAYS, and mailed them to all the newspapers. And now no one will speak to me!"

"Is that everything?" Doc asked.

"No. Someone sent emails to my colleagues and friends, making fun of them and insulting them," I told her.

"I see," Doc said.

"And there's more!" I went on. "**Someone** even inserted ***spelling*** and **GRAMMATICAL** mistakes into the manuscript of my new book. And **WORST** of all, someone used my credit card to purchase an enormouse amount of useless and EXPENSIVE items. Now I am broke, and my banker tells me that I will have to sell *The Rodent's Gazette*!"

I burst into tears.

"I AM RUINED!" I wailed, and then I began sobbing uncontrollably.

"Get ahold of yourself, Stilton," Doc said firmly. "You'll sink this ship with your tears!"

Then she took out a box labeled "Extremely Desperate Cases" and handed me a soft tissue.

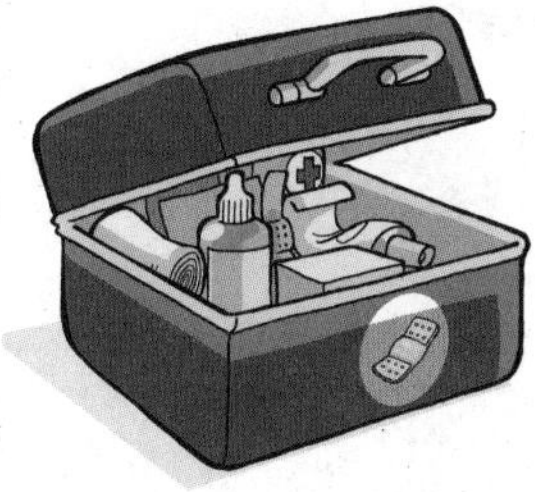

"I know things look GRIM, Stilton, but keep your snout up," she said. "This is a BAD CASE, but I've seen worse. We'll figure this out."

Doc's words gave me confidence. I stopped crying. "Thanks, Doc. Just let me know what I need to do."

She smiled. "Much better Stilton," she exclaimed. "Now hand me your laptop . . ."

I obeyed.

"Follow me!" she said, and we all went to a small research lab next to the meeting room.

Doc put my laptop on a table that looked like an operating table, with a bright light overhead. She pulled a MASK over her snout, put on a pair of latex gloves, and then opened the laptop and began to EXAMINE it.

She started typing on the keyboard. The screen lit up, and weird CODES, numbers, and letters began to scroll really fast.

Doc didn't say anything. She kept on

typing and mumbling to herself.

"Hmm . . ."

"What? What is going on?" I asked.

"Hmm . . . hmm . . ."

"What?"

"Hmm . . . hmm . . . hmm . . ."

"What what what?"

"Hmmmmmmm . . ."

After an hour of "hmm . . . hmm . . . hmm . . ." I couldn't take it anymore.

"Please, Doc, have MERCY on me and tell me something. How bad is it?" I asked.

"Hmm . . . hmm . . . hmm . . . It's bad. I mean, it's really bad. Actually, it's extremely bad!"

"Extremely bad?" I WAILED. "What happened? Please tell me!" My whiskers began to tremble from anxiety.

"What happened is that you did not

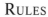

create a PASSWORD for your computer, Stilton! I knew you had forgotten the ten Golden Rules!" she replied. "So, someone accessed your laptop, stole your photos, edited them, and mailed them to the newspapers. Then they hacked into your email account and used your credit card. Basically, someone wants to destroy you, but you certainly made it easier for them, Stilton!"

Benjamin's eyes were wide open with worry. "Who could have done that?" he asked.

Thea tenderly patted his head. "That's EXACTLY what we need to find out, Benjamin," she said.

"I think I know which rotten rodent is

behind this," Doc said. "It's got to be Nick Nobody, the most NOTORIOUS hacker on Mouse Island! There isn't a single mainframe he hasn't hacked into."

Benjamin jumped up. "I know him!" he squeaked. "I play a live online video game called **Pirates of the Squeaky Seas**! Nick Nobody is the best player of that game. He's undefeated!"

"Well done, Benjamin!" Doc exclaimed. "That is a GOOD CLUE that may lead us to him!"

"Come," she said, waving her paw. "We must go to my **lab**."

NAME: NOBODY KNOWS HIS REAL NAME!

WHO HE IS: NOBODY HAS EVER SEEN HIM, BUT HE IS THE MOST WELL-KNOWN HACKER ON MOUSE ISLAND.

NICKNAME: HE LIKES TO BE CALLED NICK NOBODY.

JOB: HE IS KNOWN TO BE THE MOST TERRIFYING CYBER CRIMINAL.

WHEN HE MET GERONIMO: TO BE HONEST, NOBODY KNOWS IF THEY EVEN MET AT ALL.

HIS PASSION: HE IS FASCINATED WITH ALL ASPECTS OF COMPUTERS.

HIS SPECIALTY: HE IS A MASTER OF ONLINE VIRTUAL REALITY VIDEO GAMES.

HIS LONGTIME DREAM: HE WANTS TO FINALLY BREAK INTO THE VSSMS (VERY SECRET SUPERSECRET MOUSELY SERVICE) COMPUTER SYSTEM. GERONIMO IS A MEMBER OF THE VERY SECRET SUPERSECRET MOUSELY SERVICE AND HIS CODE NAME IS 00G.

WHAT HE LOOKS LIKE: NOBODY HAS EVER SEEN HIM.

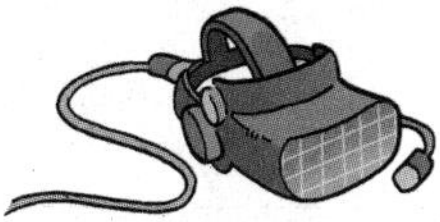

WHO'S AFRAID OF NICK NOBODY?

The lab was full of quietly humming computers, and large screens as THIN as slices of Swiss cheese hanging on walls like POSTERS.

"This is my secret research lab!" Doc proudly declared. "And these are the most powerful computers on Mouse Island! Here I store all the newest software and latest technology."

She lowered her voice. "Everything you see here is CONFIDENTIAL. You must promise me that you will not tell anyone."

"We cross our whiskers!" the three of us promised.

"Good!" Doc said. "Let's get started."

I **JUMPED** up, ready to go. "Sure, let's get busy! Let's do this!" I cried. "So . . . what are we doing, **EXACTLY**?"

"Well, I have a plan in mind," Doc said. "And a lot of it **HINGES** on you, Stilton, although I'm not sure if that's the best idea. You seem to be **totally hopeless** with computers."

"That is true," I admitted.

"But I'm afraid it's the only way," she said. "So here it is: you, Geronimo Stilton, will challenge **Nick Nobody** to his favorite game, **Pirates of the Squeaky Seas**!"

"M-m-me?" I stammered. "Challenge Nick Nobody?"

"That's right," Doc replied.

I turned as **PALE** as mozzarella. "B-b-but . . ."

"While you keep him busy, I'll try to

figure out where on Mouse Island he connects to the Internet," Doc said. "And then we will go and find him!"

"That could work!" Thea exclaimed.

"It's a good plan, except for one thing," I said. "I am not good at video games! My paws can't work the controller fast enough! I get a headache! I always forget the rules! I am totally hopeless!"

Doc opened a cabinet and pulled out GOGGLES and some strange-looking gloves.

"Don't you worry, Stilton," Doc said. "This high-tech equipment will give you the edge you need. This gear would make even the worst player look like an **EXPERT**!"

Thea's eyes were wide. "This stuff looks **cool**. What does it do?"

Doc grinned. "This gear is designed to give the player the **ULTIMATE** virtual reality experience!" she replied.

"I'm not really sure what **virtual reality** is," I admitted.

VIRTUAL REALITY

Virtual reality is a computer-created artificial world that players can interact with. Some virtual reality video games require the use of goggles with internal screens, gloves with special sensors, and headsets that feed sounds and instructions to the player. Players feel like they are inside the game!

"It's a computer-generated world designed to look real," Doc explained. "With this gear, you will feel like you are really inside the game. You'll be in a 3-D environment that you can SEE from all angles. You can hear noises and even touch things."

"What if I make mistakes?" I asked.

"Benjamin and Thea will go with you," Doc replied. "That is, if they agree. The experience will be very INTENSE and could even be DANGEROUS."

"I'll do it!" Benjamin squeaked. "I know this GAME like the back of my paw. I can guide us through it."

"I think it will be FUN," Thea added, putting on her gloves.

"Doc, how d-d-dangerous will it get?" I asked.

"If you stay calm, you won't have any

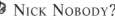

problems," Doc replied. "Everything in the world is computer-generated, so it can't HURT you. But if you forget that, well . . . you could get a very DANGEROUS scare!"

"I am not very good at staying calm," I admitted. "I think it's best if I just go home!"

"Geronimo, don't you want to get out of this MESS?" Thea asked me.

"Of course!" I said.

"Then put on your gear," my sister said firmly.

I knew she was right. I put on my headset, goggles, and the gloves.

And then I panicked! I was suddenly transported into a glowing, empty room! I didn't like the feeling one bit.

I tried to run away, but I forgot that the helmet and gloves were attached to lots of hanging cables and wires. So I tripped, rolled down the stairs, bumped my head, and ended up tangled in cables and wires!

How embarrassing!

It took Doc an hour to untangle me . . .

DEALING WITH VIRTUAL REALITY!
1
The virtual reality world freaked me out, so I decided to run away, but . . .
2
I tripped over my own paws . . .

3
I rolled down the stairs . . .

4
and I ended up tangled in cables and wires!

Like a Zombie Toad . . .

When she finished, Doc sighed. "Now that I've **untangled** Stilton, we can start," she announced.

"I hope you can **keep your cool** this time, Ger," Thea said to me. "Don't try to run away again."

My furry cheeks turned **PINK**. "I'll try to stay calm, I promise," I said. "But you know me. I can be a totally hopeless scaredy-mouse sometimes! I can't help it!"

Thea sighed. "You've got to keep it together, Brother. You don't want to **lose** *The Rodent's Gazette*, do you?"

Thea knew exactly what to say to me. Thinking of losing my beloved newspaper made me realize that I *had* to stay calm! I could not be the same old scaredy-mouse I usually was.

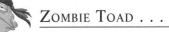

No, this time I would have to be a different kind of rodent: brave, fearless, strong, smart, fast . . .

I had to do it to save *The Rodent's Gazette*. So I took a deep breath and imagined myself as a totally different mouse.

What a fearless mouse I am!

Then I heard Doc's voice in my headset. "Benjamin, can you explain the rules of the game to Thea and Geronimo?" she asked.

"Sure!" Benjamin squeaked. As he read the rules aloud, images FLASHED inside my goggles.

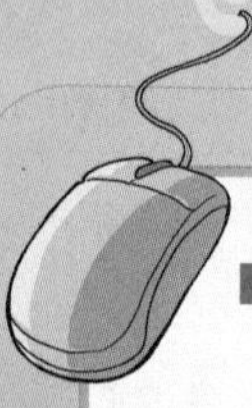

PIRATES OF THE SQUEAKY SEAS RULES OF THE GAME

This is a team game that takes place in a pirate world, with traps, attacks, and treasures to be found. The object of the game is for each team to reach its own treasure island. Each player has nine lives. After the ninth life, the player is eliminated. Players lose a life every time they are hit. When any of the members of a team lose their nine lives, the team is automatically eliminated, too. During the game, it is essential to stock up on food, weapons, water, and treasures to keep going in the game.

1. *Pirates of the Squeaky Seas* is a multiplayer online game.
2. Each team is named after a pirate ship. Each player can choose his/her own name and choose his/her own character.
3. The game consists of ten levels. Each level has tasks of varying difficulties. In order to advance to the next level, you have to successfully complete all the tasks.

LEVEL 1: ROOKIE
LEVEL 2: MATE
LEVEL 3: CREWMAN
LEVEL 4: BOATSWAIN
LEVEL 5: WOLF OF THE SEA
LEVEL 6: BUCCANEER
LEVEL 7: RAIDER
LEVEL 8: PRIVATEER
LEVEL 9: PIRATE ON THE ATTACK
LEVEL 10: CORSAIR OF THE SEVEN SEAS

Only Nick Nobody has reached Level 10. No player has ever defeated him.

"Is everything clear, Uncle Ger?" Benjamin asked when he had finished explaining the rules. "The first few LEVELS are pretty easy, so you should be able to figure it out as you go. But first we have to choose the name of our pirate ship and create our CHARACTERS. Any suggestions?"

I pondered this for a bit. "We could name our ship Scrolling Surfer, just like Doc's ship. What do you think? And I will be GERRY SHIVERTAIL."

"And I will be Terry the Terrible!" Thea announced.

"And I will be Benny the Buccaneer!" Benjamin added.

Then we got to select eyes, snouts, ears, WHISKERS, noses, clothing, and accessories from the screen to create our character looks. Here is what we came up with . . .

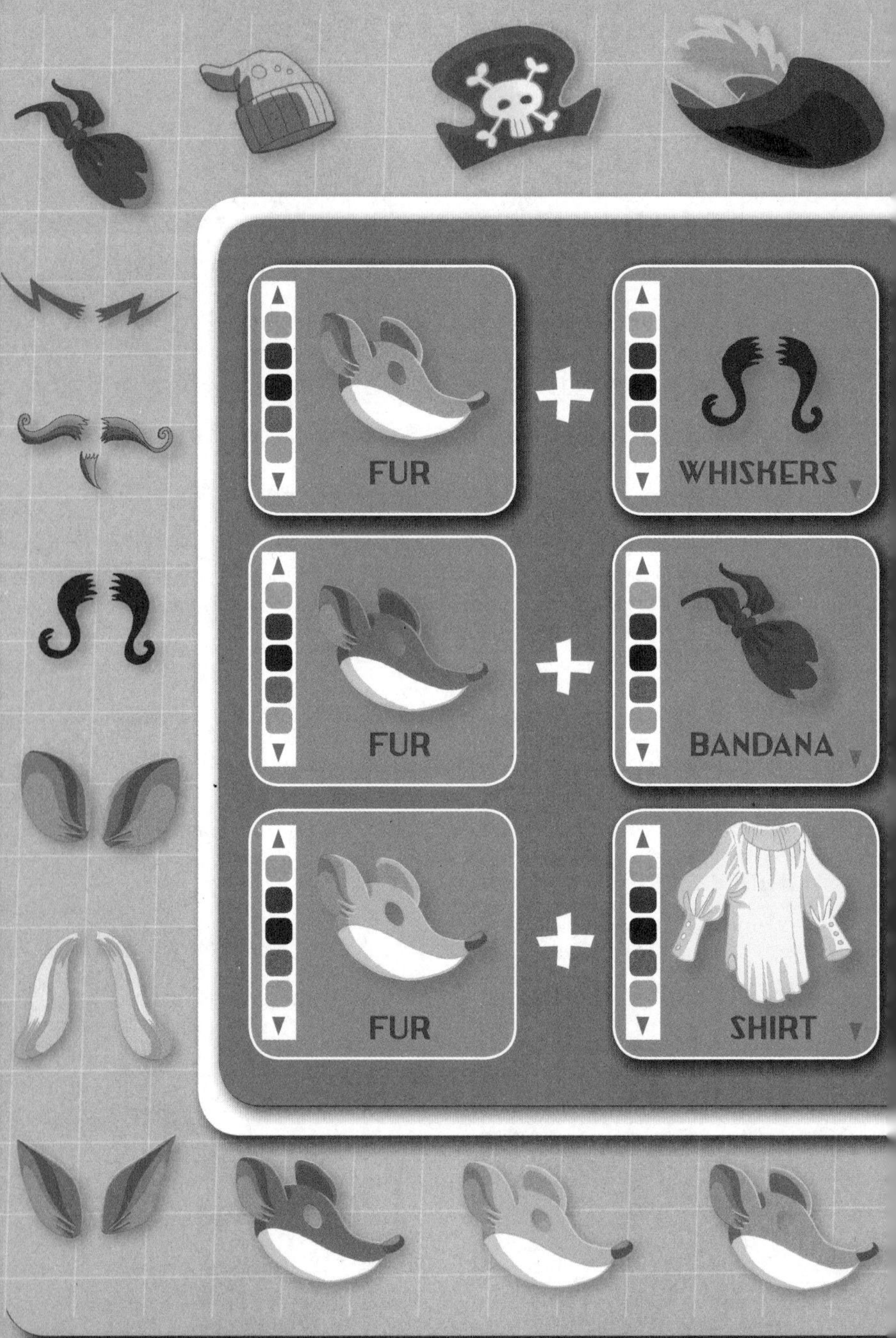
FUR
WHISKERS
FUR
BANDANA
FUR
SHIRT

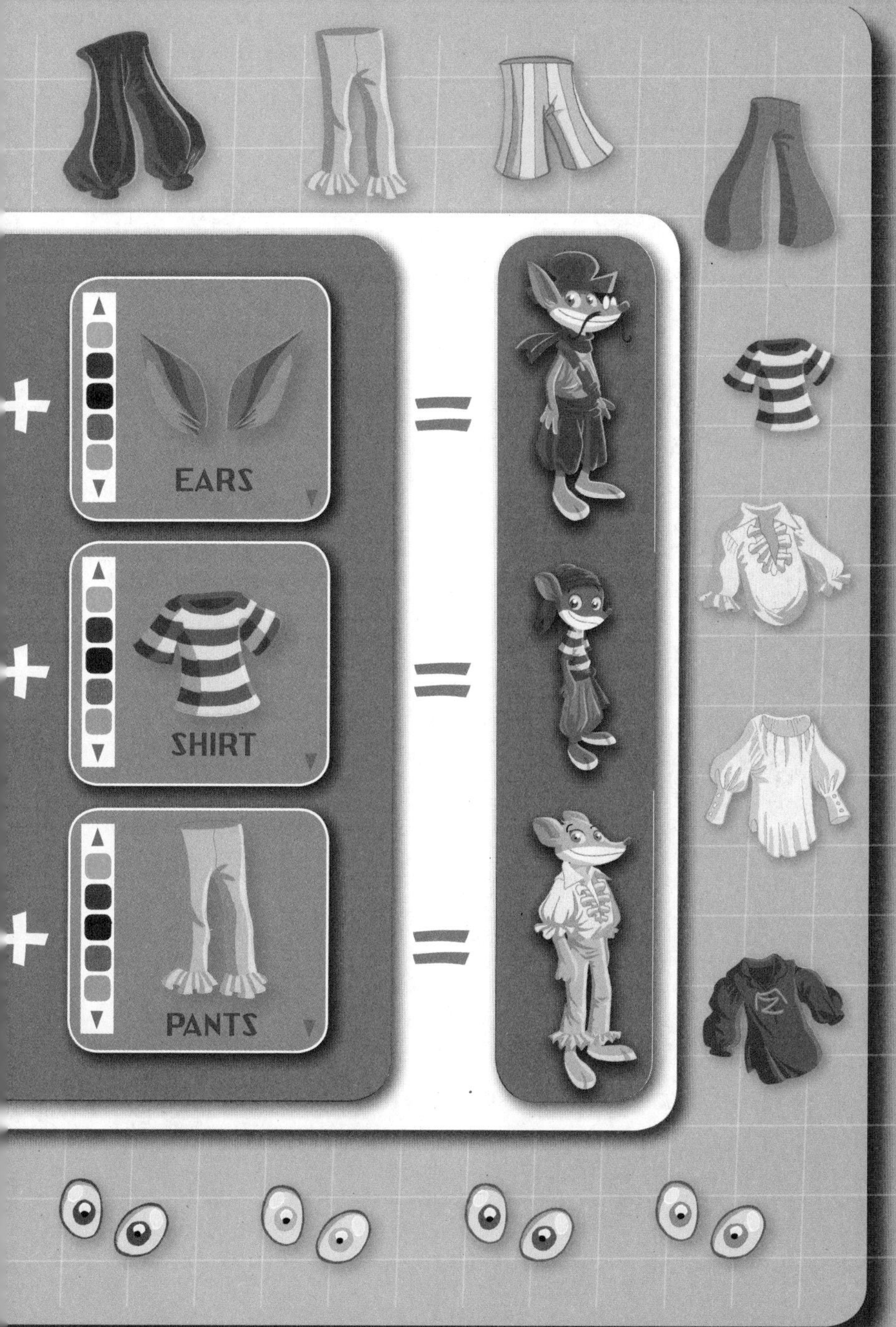
EARS
SHIRT
PANTS

We were all very happy with our characters . . . except for me! I thought the GREEN fur I chose for GERRY SHIVERTAIL would look cool. But Thea took a look at my character and giggled. "Well, at least you will SCARE our enemies! You look like a giant toad dressed up like a pirate!"

Doc looked at my character. "That COLOR is perfect, in my opinion!" she said. "It looks exactly the way you did, Stilton, when you were seasick on the ship earlier."

"I really like it, Uncle Ger!" Benjamin added. "You look like a ZOMBIE toad pirate on a ghost ship."

"I don't want to look like a

zombie toad pirate!" I cried.

"Sorry, Uncle Ger, but I've already uploaded our characters," Benjamin said.

"Then it's time to BEGIN our mission," Doc said. "Make sure your goggles are firmly in place. Remember that there are WIRES attached to your gloves, and don't make any big movements. Now, if you're ready . . . OFF YOU GO! Good luck, everyone!"

The screen inside my goggles FLASHED, and suddenly everything changed. We were inside the **Pirates of the Squeaky Seas** game! It was incredible! It really looked like were on board on old pirate ship! The ship was **anchored** off the shore of an island.

"The first four levels are pretty simple," Benjamin explained. "We need to bring supplies from the **shore** onto the ship."

We quickly advanced through the first four levels. We carried chests full of GOLD DOUBLOONS on board, and barrels full of oily ANCHOVIES that we could actually smell! (They were very stinky!)

"You'll never know what you might need in the game," explained Benja — I mean, BENNY THE BUCCANEER. "And now, we can set sail!"

Terry the Terrible (my sister, and our ship's captain) hoisted the anchor, and we sailed into the blue ocean — and the FIFTH LEVEL of the game. Soon we spotted a PIRATE SHIP sailing toward us with black sails.

Then . . . BOOM! The pirate ship fired one of its cannons at us!

"PREPARE TO BE ATTACKED!" Benny the Buccaneer shouted.

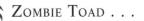

It's Only a Video Game!

The cannonball splashed in the water just a few feet from the ship. The waves rocked, and I started to feel seasick.

Then the wind began to **BLOW** so violently that we were scared it would tear apart the sails.

BOOM! A second cannonball flew toward us, narrowly missing us again.

"Quick, lower the sails!" Thea ordered.

I pulled at the ropes, but they were **tangled** up at the top of the mainmast.

"Climb up there, Gerry Shivertail!" Benjamin called out.

I gulped. *It's only a video game,* I told myself, and I **CLIMBED** up the tall mast.

Then I made the mistake of looking down. The deck looked like it was far, far below me! I got super dizzy! My head began to spin like a wheel of cheese!

Then I heard a gentle voice in my ear.

"IT'S ONLY A VIDEO GAME, STILTON . . . don't forget that . . . it's only a video game!"

It was Doc! She was WATCHING us on a computer screen, so she knew everything that was happening to us.

The sound of her voice helped to calm me down.

I took a deep breath and **untangled** the ropes. Our ship sailed away from the attacking ship . . . and we advanced to the sixth level!

"**Way to go, Gerry Shivertail!**" Thea cheered.

But we could not celebrate for long, because the pirate ship with the **black sails** pulled up next to us. Terrifying pirates waving swords tried to board our ship!

"Uh-oh," said Benjamin. "We forgot to stock up on weapons!"

"Well, we Stiltons are peaceful mice," Thea said.

"But what do we do now?" I asked. "How will we fight back?"

Once again we heard Doc's voice in our ears: "**IT'S ONLY A VIDEO GAME.** They can't hurt you."

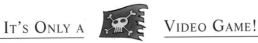

Benjamin was the first to calm down. He ran to the galley, took a barrel of the oily anchovies, and spilled them on the deck! Thea and I did the same and overturned two more barrels of the super-stinky, oily, and SLIMY anchovies.

When the attacking pirates jumped on our ship's deck, they slipped on the stinky anchovies. They all fell overboard,

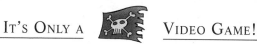

splashing right into a school of hungry sharks! The sharks chased them away.

Then we advanced to the SEVENTH LEVEL.

Levels 7 and 8 were fairly easy. No other ships ATTACKED us. We sailed the seas, stocking up on points and chests of GOLD DOUBLOONS.

I was almost relaxed when we got to the NINTH LEVEL. Maybe the video game was not as **difficult** as I thought it would be!

And then — I got distracted on an island and forgot to board the *Scrolling Surfer*. Thea and Benjamin sailed off without me.

That's when I got into big trouble. I lost seven out of my nine lives!

I got **poked** by a sharp sword. (-1 life)

I FELL into a swamp of hungry alligators. (-1 life)

I was **captured** by the enemy pirates. (-1 life)

The pirates were ANGRY, so they fed me to the sharks. (-1 lives)

Before the sharks could eat me, a whale SWALLOWED me. (-1 life)

The whale hiccupped me back out onto a deserted ISLAND. (-1 life)

HOW I LOST SEVEN LIVES . . .

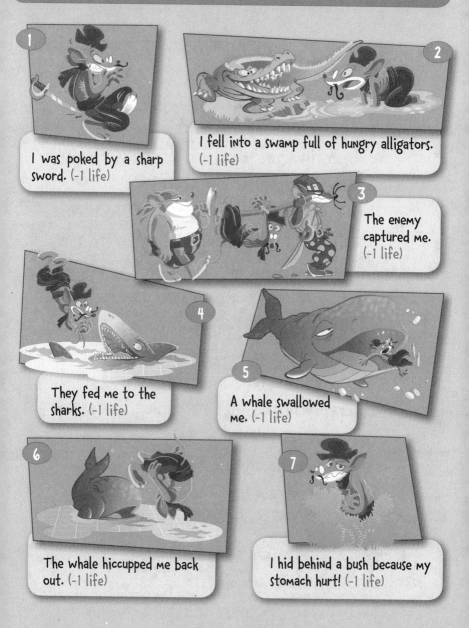

I was poked by a sharp sword. (-1 life)

I fell into a swamp full of hungry alligators. (-1 life)

The enemy captured me. (-1 life)

They fed me to the sharks. (-1 life)

A whale swallowed me. (-1 life)

The whale hiccupped me back out. (-1 life)

I hid behind a bush because my stomach hurt! (-1 life)

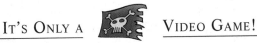

There was nothing to eat there, so I **chomped** on wild berries and had such a bad stomachache that I had to hide behind the bushes for hours! (-1 life)

What a disaster. Because of me my team was about to get **eliminated**!

Then I heard Doc's voice again. "Remember, **IT'S ONLY A VIDEO GAME**!" she said. "You don't really have a stomachache! Use your brains and try to find your teammates."

Doc's words **calmed** me down once again. I thought up a plan.

I wrote a message to my friends and put it in an empty bottle that I found. I threw the bottle in the ocean.

I had done the right thing!

A happy melody started playing:

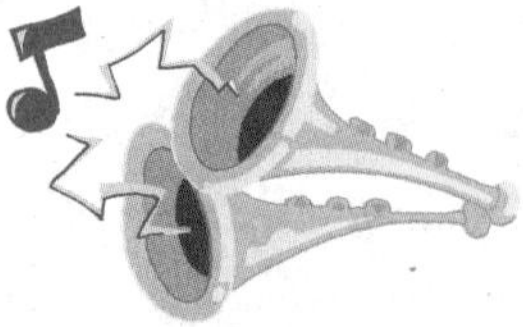

BA DA DA BA BA
BAAAAA!

I started jumping up and down. I had made it to the TENTH LEVEL!

The game instantly *transported* me to the *Scrolling Surfer.* Thea had the bottle in her paw.

"We LOOKED for you everywhere!" she scolded. "Where were you, Gerry Shivertail?"

"Sorry, Captain Terrible, but I got lost," I replied. "I had to fight off SHARKS, WHALES, and alligators!"

Then I frowned. "I'm so sorry, but I lost seven of my nine lives! I have only two left!"

"Don't worry, GERRY SHIVERTAIL!" Benjamin said. "The important thing is that we are all back together. We are a team and we can win if we STICK TOGETHER. We won't lose you again!"

That made me feel better. "Thanks,

BENNY THE BUCCANEER!" I said.

Thea tapped my shoulder and pointed off the deck of the ship. "**Nick Nobody's island** is over there. All we have to do is get there, **battle** him, and win. Is everybody ready?"

"**READY, CAPTAIN!**" Benjamin and I shouted in reply.

"Then let's go show that **hacker** that nobody messes with the Stiltons!" Thea cheered.

My Name Is Nick Nobody!

We lowered a SMALL BOAT in the water and ROWED toward the island. Suddenly, three boats full of PIRATES came toward us from behind a ROCKY ridge! Squeak! We were in trouble!

The captain was a SCRAWNY mouse. He had parrot on his shoulder, an eye patch, and wore a large pirate hat with a gold letter *N*. *N* for Nick Nobody!

He looked me up and down. "You, with the moldy green–colored fur!" he called out.

"Who, me?" I replied, my WHISKERS trembling.

"Yes, you!" he barked. "Do you see anyone

else with moldy **GREEN** fur?"

"N-n-no sir," I stammered.

"Congratulations! You are **VERY SCARY**!" he said. "You look like a ***ZOMBIE TOAD*** dressed up like a pirate."

"Um, pleased to meet you," I said, not sure if he was complimenting me or not. "M-my name is Geron . . . I mean, GERRY SHIVERTAIL. And who are you?"

"My name is Nick, **Nick Nobody**!" he replied. "Do you want to know why?

Because until now NOBODY has been able to find me, NOBODY has been able to defeat me, and NOBODY ever will, is that clear? Especially not a cheesehead with moldy green FUR and two **rookies**."

"I am no rookie. I am **Terry the Terrible**, the captain of this crew," Thea announced boldly. "We are here to compete against you!"

Nick Nobody burst out laughing. "You cannot defeat me! NOBODY can!" he boasted.

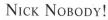

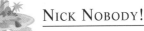

"I created this game! I came up with its tricks, deceptions, and traps. I made sure that I am the only one who can win. Only me! Always only me!"

The parrot on his shoulder shrieked, "Only him, always only him!"

"Aren't you ashamed of yourself?" Benjamin asked him. "That's not fair. That's cheating!"

I hate to lose!
He hates to lose!

Nick Nobody shrugged. "Well, I don't care. **I HATE TO LOSE!**"

"**He hates to lose!**" the parrot repeated.

"Quiet, you pipsqueak, or else I'll use your tail fathers to decorate my hat!" Nick scolded the parrot.

"**Quiet you pipsqueak, quiet you pipsqueak!**" the parrot shrieked, flying off.

Then the parrot landed on my shoulder.

"You **feathery** traitor!" Nick Nobody yelled.

Then he turned to his crew. "I am done talking to this SCRAWNY band of pirates. It's time to attack!"

"**Attack! Attack!**" the parrot repeated.

Nick Nobody's pirates rowed really ***fast*** toward our dinghy. Then they started RAMMING their boats into ours! Our dinghy **tipped over** and we fell into the water!

We had each lost one life! I was down to just one. As we were gasping for air, we could hear Doc's voice in our ears.

"Don't forget, it's only a video game!" she told us. "You can still breathe underwater."

Of course! That made sense. We all started to breathe normally.

I LOOKED around at the underwater plants and rocks. I spotted a ray of LIGHT coming through a rock covered in seaweed and sea anemone. As I got closer, I realized that the HOLE in the rock was an opening to an underwater tunnel!

I signaled to Thea and Benjamin to follow me and we swam into the CAVE. We swam and swam to the center of the island — we were about to reach Nick Nobody's hideout!

"This is it, Gerry Shivertail!" Benjamin called out. "LEVEL 10. We just have to take over the hideout and we'll win the game!"

"Hooray!" I cheered. "I can't wait to show that smarty-mouse Nick Nobody that we're not pathetic, scrawny pirates. Let's take the hideout!"

I turned to run into the hideout — and found myself snout-to-snout with a VICIOUS-LOOKING shark.

He opened his huge mouth, filled with SHARP teeth.

"Squeeeeeeak, help! A SHARK!" I wailed. I was about to lose my last life!

Just as the virtual

shark began to gobble me up, I heard Doc's voice in my ears.

"Hang on! I am taking you back to the REAL WORLD," she said. "Three . . . two . . . one . . . HERE WE GO!"

The image of the shark's TERRIFYING mouth disappeared, replaced by a blue screen. Whew! I was glad that was over.

But it meant that Nick Nobody had won the game . . .

Who Is the Real Nick Nobody?

After a few minutes, we were back on Doc's ship. We were completely out of it and feeling **dizzy**, **dizzy**, **dizzy**!

I took off my goggles, my headset, and my gloves and immediately checked the color of my own fur.

I was happy to see that it was no longer the moldy green color of a zombie toad!

We were back in the real world!

Doc happily hugged us.

"You all did great!" she congratulated us. "And thanks to your hard work, I have figured out where Nick Nobody is hiding!"

She showed us a map of Mouse Island, with a RED X right off the coast of the Sea of Mice.

We climbed back up to the MAIN DECK and joined Uncle Grayfur at the WHEEL of the *Scrolling Surfer.*

"Doc, we're almost

at the SPOT on the map. But your big RED X is on the water. There is no island at that location. Are you sure that's the place?"

"ABSOLUTELY, Captain. That's the spot!" Doc replied.

I borrowed Uncle Grayfur's binoculars and SCANNED the sea surface.

I noticed a little green dot on the horizon.

"Land!" I screamed.

"And it looks just like Nick Nobody's

hideout in the virtual reality game," Benjamin remarked.

"He must have found an uncharted ISLAND for his hideout," Doc guessed.

"HOORAY!" Thea cheered. "Now we can take down that rotten hacker!"

"Yeah! He's more rotten than ten-year-old cheese!" Benjamin added.

I did not know whether to be happy or terrified. Nick Nobody was a skilled hacker who did not want to be found. I was positive that the entire island would be protected by a sophisticated SECURITY system. There might be LASER RAYS capable of frying off our whiskers, I imagined.

How scary! I really like my whiskers!

Then it hit me: there might be a safer way to get to Nick's hideout.

"What if there is an underwater tunnel

leading to the hideout, just like in the game?" I asked. "We could take that and sneak into the hideout."

"Brilliant, Stilton!" Doc said. "Let's get suited up!"

Uncle Grayfur dropped anchor off the coast of the island. Doc, Thea, and I put on wet suits, masks, and oxygen tanks. Then we JUMPED into the water, while Benjamin and my uncle stayed behind.

We swam through seaweed and rocks. Then I saw a ray of LIGHT, just like in the game. We had reached the underwater tunnel! We swam inside. As we got deeper and deeper into the cave, I had a feeling that I was forgetting something.

Nick Nobody's hideout looked just like the one in the game. The tunnel was the same. So at the end of the tunnel we would probably find a . . .

Shark! I screamed inside my head. A huge SHARK with SHARP teeth was about to bite off my tail! And this was no VIRTUAL shark. It was real!

How could I forget about the shark in the video game? I made my escape by

quickly swimming into a narrow crawl space. Doc and Thea followed me.

After a few feet, however, we found ourselves in very nasty SLIME. To escape the shark, we had swum right into the sewer pipe! Thankfully, we were wearing the oxygen tanks, otherwise we would have fainted from the smell!

I should have let that shark gobble *me up!* I thought.

Luckily, Doc found a metal LADDER leading out of the slime. She motioned for us to follow her. When we reached the top, we very quietly pushed up a metal grate and ended up . . . inside Nick Nobody's **secret hideout**!

The metal bunker was filled with computers and screens, all busy running code. We tiptoed across the floor. Nick Nobody had his back to us and was playing **Pirates of the Squeaky Seas**, which, of course, he was winning.

Thea charged at him. "This time you lose, Nick Nobody!" she cried.

Thea **swiveled** Nick's chair, and the hacker became tied up in all of the game's **WIRES** and cables.

"How dare you!" he squeaked. "I am Nick Nobody. Nobody can defeat me!"

"Well, **SOMEBODY** has defeated you, and it's us!" Doc told him. "You rotten cheater!"

I noticed that Nick Nobody was wearing a costume. He wore a captain's suit and a pirate hat. His hair covered one eye.

"You really take this game very seriously, don't you?" I asked.

"You don't know what you're talking about, old mouse!" Nick Nobody said.

"OLD MOUSE!" I squeaked. "I'm not really that old. If I have any gray whiskers it's because I work so hard at *The Rodent's Gazette*."

"Geronimo!" Thea screamed. "Focus!"

"Right." I turned my attention back to Nick Nobody.

"Can you please explain why you broke into MY computer, stole MY photos, used MY credit card, and spent all MY money?" I asked, my voice getting louder with each word.

Got you!
Argh!

Ummm . . .
But is that him?

He chuckled, pleased with himself, and his hat slipped off his head. Nick Nobody was no more than a young mouselet, wearing a costume and a wig! "Stilton, you CHEESEBRAIN, you made it really easy for me!" he replied. "You didn't have a PASSWORD for your computer! No password for your email account, either!"

"I didn't ask you HOW you did it, I asked WHY!" I yelled desperately. "Why, why, why?

Because of you I might lose *The Rodent's Gazette*! The newspaper that my grandfather worked all his life for! My colleagues will lose their jobs! And THOUSANDS of young **readers** will have to give up reading the **BOOKS** they love so much that stimulate their imaginations!"

Nick Nobody frowned. "**BOOKS** that stimulate your imagination?"

"Yes," I replied. "I am a writer, as you know. Or I should say, I was one, until you ruined everything!"

The young hacker got a far-off look in his eyes. "I remember . . . when I was a little **mousekin**, I used to read a lot," he said. "I loved adventure books, especially the ones about PIRATES. Then, slowly, I became more and more interested in video games and computers. I stopped reading."

"But why?" I asked. "Reading is a wonderful activity!"

He started to CRY. "I miss those BOOKS! And now other mousekins won't get to read your books, and it's all my fault!"

I sighed. "Yes, I'm afraid it is."

"What can I do to FIX this?" he asked.

"It's too late," I replied. "I am broke. My reputation is ruined. And nobody loves me anymore!"

All's Well That Ends Well!

We **UNTIED** Nick Nobody, who was **sorry** for what he did. Then we called Benjamin and told him to ask Uncle Grayfur to come over with the ship and take us back **home**.

During the trip back to New Mouse City, I fell into a deep sleep.

I woke up many hours later, when I heard a

strange sound. It was cheerful music, played by a band.

I opened my eyes and JUMPED up. The harbor of New Mouse City was filled with rodents! What I SAW left me squeakless . . .

As soon as we got off the ship, reporters from every TV network and Internet news show on Mouse Island surrounded us.

"Mr. Stilton, tell us your story!"

"We want to know everything, from beginning to end!"

I was about to reply, but before I could utter a squeak, Nick Nobody came forward.

"Good rodents, I would like to make a statement," he said in his high, squeaky voice. "Everybody knows me as Nick Nobody, but my real name is Shaky Fraidy.

"I am — actually, I was — a hacker, a notorious cyber criminal. In fact, I was the most feared hacker anywhere! I did some pretty awful things. I snooped around other mice's computers. I SPIED and I caused all sorts of trouble."

"You can say that again," Doc muttered.

"I never stole anything," Nick went on. "I just did it to prove that I was the best. That nobody could DEFEAT me. But I went TOO FAR with Mr. Stilton."

"You can say *that* again," I added.

Nick continued his confession. "I took some of his PHOTOS, edited them, and sent them to newspapers," he admitted. "I pretended to be him and sent mean emails signed with his name. Then I bought a lot of useless and EXPENSIVE items using his credit card. In other words . . . it's all my fault! Mr. Stilton is a real gentlemouse!"

Mr. Moneypaws stepped forward. "Mr.

What a welcome back!
Ummm . . .
It's them!

They're here!
HOORAY!
Yay!
Hooray!
OME BACK!

Stilton, we understand that you were not the one who made all those purchases," he said. "The merchants are willing to take everything back."

I sighed with relief.

Then my coworkers at *The Rodent's Gazette* stepped forward.

"Boss, we should have known that you wouldn't have sent us such NASTY messages," Ms. Raven said. "We're sorry we JUMPED to conclusions."

Then it was Grandpa William's turn. "Grandson, I am sorry that I had doubts about you," he said. "I now understand that you would never jeopardize *The Rodent's Gazette*! I admire you and **love you** very much, even though I don't say it very often!"

I was TEARING UP from the emotion I was feeling. Everything was back to the way it was! I wasn't going to lose the newspaper. And everyone liked me again!

Then the mayor called me onto a stage. "Geronimo Stilton, today you have brought to justice a dangerous cyber criminal!" he said. "I am awarding you with this MEDAL OF HONOR: the Defender of the City. This is the same medal that was awarded to those brave rodents who fought off an attack of FIERCE pirates many years ago."

Then he draped a GOLD medal around my neck!

The band began to play the anthem of New Mouse City. I sang along at the top of my lungs, with a paw on my heart and eyes full of tears.

Then I spoke: "Distinguished Mayor, I am

not alone in deserving this honor," I said. "The mice who helped me deserve it as well: my sister, THEA; my nephew Benjamin; my uncle Grayfur; and Professor Margo Bitmouse!"

The mayor asked them to come to the stage and awarded them all, too. When all the awards were given, the crowd began to cheer.

"What can we do to thank you?" the mayor asked us.

To the Defender of the City!
What an honor!

I **huddled** with Thea and Doc. Then I turned to the mayor.

"We don't need a reward, but there is one thing you can do, Mr. Mayor," I said. "Please do not send Nick Nobody — I mean, Shaky Fraidy — to jail. He is sorry for what he did. To make up for the trouble he caused, he can help us write a **BOOK** about surfing the web safely and avoiding **HACKERS** like him! After all, he is an expert on the subject!"

"**Excellent** idea!" the mayor agreed.

So Shaky Fraidy helped Doc and me write the book, and it was a great **success**! You could say that my story had a REAL happy ending — not a VIRTUAL one!

Yours truly, Stilton, *Geronimo Stilton*!

Be sure to read all my fabumouse adventures!

#1 Lost Treasure of the Emerald Eye

#2 The Curse of the Cheese Pyramid

#3 Cat and Mouse in a Haunted House

#4 I'm Too Fond of My Fur!

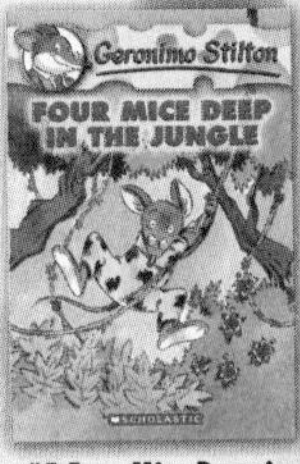

#5 Four Mice Deep in the Jungle

#6 Paws Off, Cheddarface!

#7 Red Pizzas for a Blue Count

#8 Attack of the Bandit Cats

#9 A Fabumouse Vacation for Geronimo

#10 All Because of a Cup of Coffee

#11 It's Halloween, You 'Fraidy Mouse!

#12 Merry Christmas, Geronimo!

#13 The Phantom of the Subway

#14 The Temple of the Ruby of Fire

#15 The Mona Mousa Code

#16 A Cheese-Colored Camper

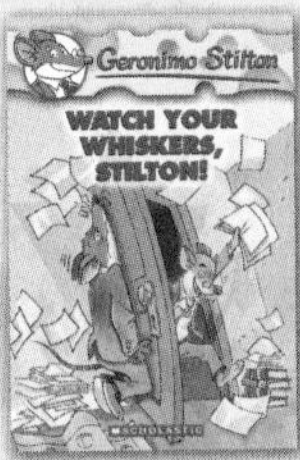

#17 Watch Your Whiskers, Stilton!

#18 Shipwreck on the Pirate Islands

#19 My Name Is Stilton, Geronimo Stilton

#20 Surf's Up, Geronimo!

#21 The Wild, Wild West

#22 The Secret of Cacklefur Castle

A Christmas Tale

#23 Valentine's Day Disaster

#24 Field Trip to Niagara Falls

#25 The Search for Sunken Treasure

#26 The Mummy with No Name

#27 The Christmas Toy Factory

#28 Wedding Crasher

#29 Down and Out Down Under

#30 The Mouse Island Marathon

#31 The Mysterious Cheese Thief

Christmas Catastrophe

#32 Valley of the Giant Skeletons

#33 Geronimo and the Gold Medal Mystery

#34 Geronimo Stilton, Secret Agent

#35 A Very Merry Christmas

#36 Geronimo's Valentine

#37 The Race Across America

#38 A Fabumouse School Adventure

#39 Singing Sensation

#40 The Karate Mouse

#41 Mighty Mount Kilimanjaro

#42 The Peculiar Pumpkin Thief

#43 I'm Not a Supermouse!

#44 The Giant Diamond Robbery

#45 Save the White Whale!

#46 The Haunted Castle

#47 Run for the Hills, Geronimo!

#48 The Mystery in Venice

#49 The Way of the Samurai

#50 This Hotel Is Haunted!

#51 The Enormouse Pearl Heist

#52 Mouse in Space!

#53 Rumble in the Jungle

#54 Get into Gear, Stilton!

#55 The Golden Statue Plot

#56 Flight of the Red Bandit

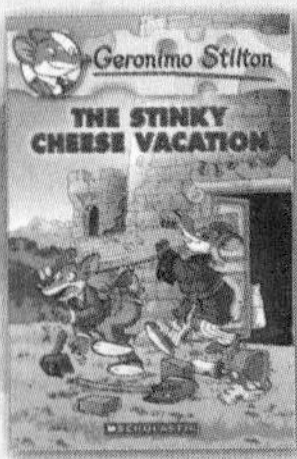

#57 The Stinky Cheese Vacation

#58 The Super Chef Contest

#59 Welcome to Moldy Manor

#60 The Treasure of Easter Island

#61 Mouse House Hunter

#62 Mouse Overboard!

#63 The Cheese Experiment

#64 Magical Mission

#65 Bollywood Burglary

#66 Operation: Secret Recipe

#67 The Chocolate Chase

#68 Cyber-Thief Showdown

Up Next:

#69 Hug a Tree, Geronimo

MEET Geronimo Stiltonord

He is a mouseking — the Geronimo Stilton of the ancient far north! He lives with his brawny and brave clan in the village of Mouseborg. From sailing frozen waters to facing fiery dragons, every day is an adventure for the micekings!

#1 Attack of the Dragons

#2 The Famouse Fjord Race

#3 Pull the Dragon's Tooth!

#4 Stay Strong, Geronimo!

#5 The Mysterious Message

#6 The Helmet Holdup

#7 The Dragon Crown

Thea Stilton and the Lost Letters

Thea Stilton and the Tropical Treasure

Thea Stilton and the Hollywood Hoax

Thea Stilton and the Madagascar Madness

Thea Stilton and the Frozen Fiasco

Thea Stilton and the Venice Masquerade

Thea Stilton and the Niagara Splash

And check out my fabumouse special editions!

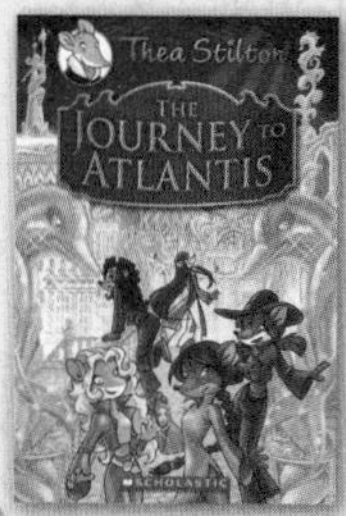

THEA STILTON: THE JOURNEY TO ATLANTIS

THEA STILTON: THE SECRET OF THE FAIRIES

THEA STILTON: THE SECRET OF THE SNOW

THEA STILTON: THE CLOUD CASTLE

THEA STILTON: THE TREASURE OF THE SEA

THEA STILTON: THE LAND OF FLOWERS

MEET GERONIMO STILTONIX

He is a spacemouse — the Geronimo Stilton of a parallel universe! He is captain of the spaceship *MouseStar 1*. While flying through the cosmos, he visits distant planets and meets crazy aliens. His adventures are out of this world!

#1 Alien Escape

#2 You're Mine, Captain!

#3 Ice Planet Adventure

#4 The Galactic Goal

#5 Rescue Rebellion

#6 The Underwater Planet

#7 Beware! Space Junk!

#8 Away in a Star Sled

#9 Slurp Monster Showdown

#10 Pirate Spacecat Attack

#11 We'll Bite Your Tail, Geronimo!

Up Next!

#12 The Invisible Planet

ABOUT THE AUTHOR

Born in New Mouse City, Mouse Island, **GERONIMO STILTON** is Rattus Emeritus of Mousomorphic Literature and of Neo-Ratonic Comparative Philosophy. For the past twenty years, he has been running *The Rodent's Gazette*, New Mouse City's most widely read daily newspaper.

Stilton was awarded the Ratitzer Prize for his scoops on *The Curse of the Cheese Pyramid* and *The Search for Sunken Treasure*. He has also received the Andersen 2000 Prize for Personality of the Year. One of his bestsellers won the 2002 eBook Award for world's best ratlings' electronic book. His works have been published all over the globe.

In his spare time, Mr. Stilton collects antique cheese rinds and plays golf. But what he most enjoys is telling stories to his nephew Benjamin.

6
5
4
3
2
1
1. Main entrance
2. Printing presses (where the books and newspaper are printed)
3. Accounts department
4. Editorial room (where the editors, illustrators, and designers work)
5. Geronimo Stilton's office
6. Helicopter landing pad
THE RODENT'S GAZETTE

1
2
3
4
5
6
7
8
9
10
11
12
13
14
15
16
17
18
19
20
21
22
23
24
25
26
27
28
29
30
31
32
33
34
35
36
37
38
39
40
41
42
43
44
45
46
RODENT RIVER
Beach

Map of New Mouse City

1. Industrial Zone
2. Cheese Factories
3. Angorat International Airport
4. WRAT Radio and Television Station
5. Cheese Market
6. Fish Market
7. Town Hall
8. Snotnose Castle
9. The Seven Hills of Mouse Island
10. Mouse Central Station
11. Trade Center
12. Movie Theater
13. Gym
14. Catnegie Hall
15. Singing Stone Plaza
16. The Gouda Theater
17. Grand Hotel
18. Mouse General Hospital
19. Botanical Gardens
20. Cheap Junk for Less (Trap's store)
21. Aunt Sweetfur and Benjamin's House
22. Mouseum of Modern Art
23. University and Library
24. *The Daily Rat*
25. *The Rodent's Gazette*
26. Trap's House
27. Fashion District
28. The Mouse House Restaurant
29. Environmental Protection Center
30. Harbor Office
31. Mousidon Square Garden
32. Golf Course
33. Swimming Pool
34. Tennis Courts
35. Curlyfur Island Amousement Park
36. Geronimo's House
37. Historic District
38. Public Library
39. Shipyard
40. Thea's House
41. New Mouse Harbor
42. Luna Lighthouse
43. The Statue of Liberty
44. Hercule Poirat's Office
45. Petunia Pretty Paws's House
46. Grandfather William's House

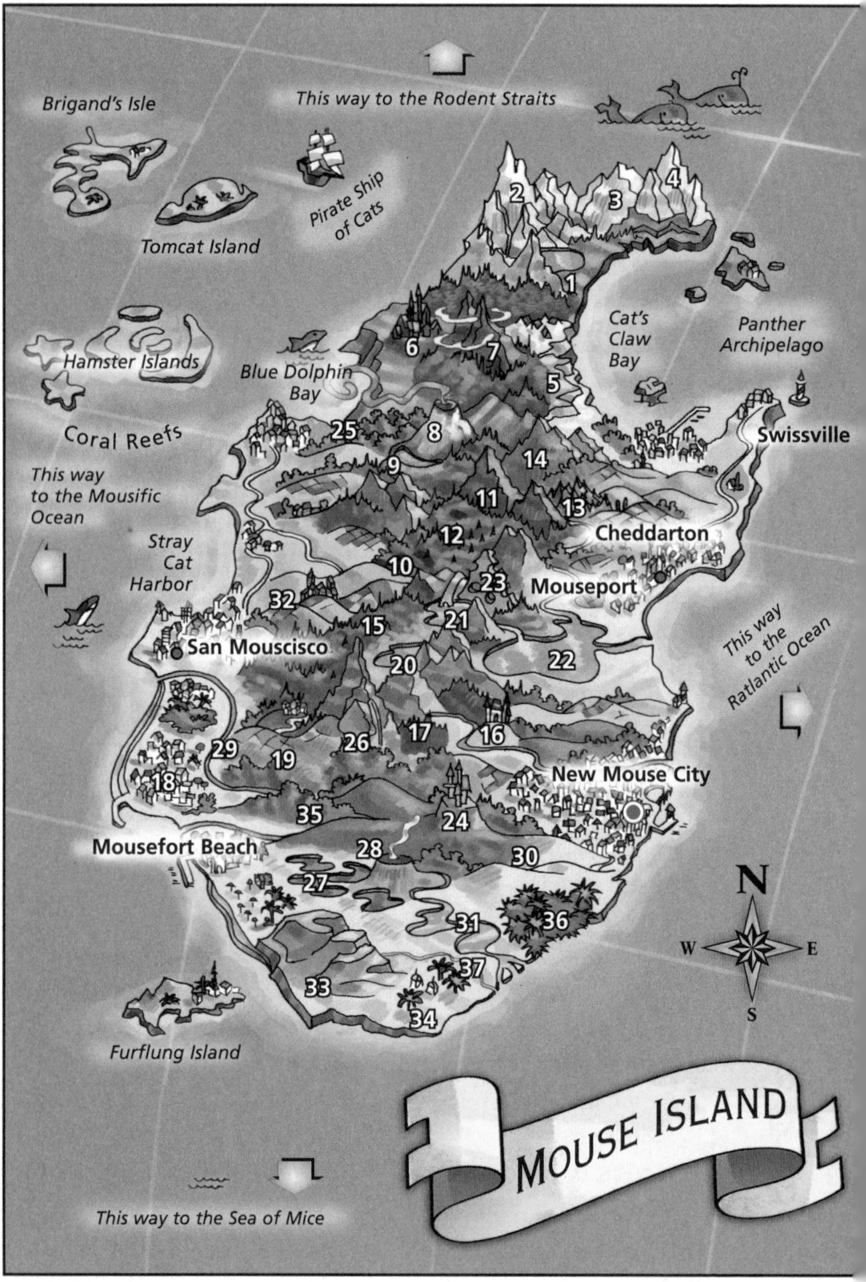

This way to the Rodent Straits
Brigand's Isle
Tomcat Island
Pirate Ship of Cats
Hamster Islands
Blue Dolphin Bay
Coral Reefs
This way to the Mousific Ocean
Stray Cat Harbor
Cat's Claw Bay
Panther Archipelago
Swissville
Cheddarton
Mouseport
San Mouscisco
This way to the Ratlantic Ocean
New Mouse City
Mousefort Beach
Furflung Island
This way to the Sea of Mice
MOUSE ISLAND
N
W
E
S
1
2
3
4
5
6
7
8
9
10
11
12
13
14
15
16
17
18
19
20
21
22
23
24
25
26
27
28
29
30
31
32
33
34
35
36
37

Map of Mouse Island

1. Big Ice Lake
2. Frozen Fur Peak
3. Slipperyslopes Glacier
4. Coldcreeps Peak
5. Ratzikistan
6. Transratania
7. Mount Vamp
8. Roastedrat Volcano
9. Brimstone Lake
10. Poopedcat Pass
11. Stinko Peak
12. Dark Forest
13. Vain Vampires Valley
14. Goose Bumps Gorge
15. The Shadow Line Pass
16. Penny Pincher Castle
17. Nature Reserve Park
18. Las Ratayas Marinas
19. Fossil Forest
20. Lake Lake
21. Lake Lakelake
22. Lake Lakelakelake
23. Cheddar Crag
24. Cannycat Castle
25. Valley of the Giant Sequoia
26. Cheddar Springs
27. Sulfurous Swamp
28. Old Reliable Geyser
29. Vole Vale
30. Ravingrat Ravine
31. Gnat Marshes
32. Munster Highlands
33. Mousehara Desert
34. Oasis of the Sweaty Camel
35. Cabbagehead Hill
36. Rattytrap Jungle
37. Rio Mosquito

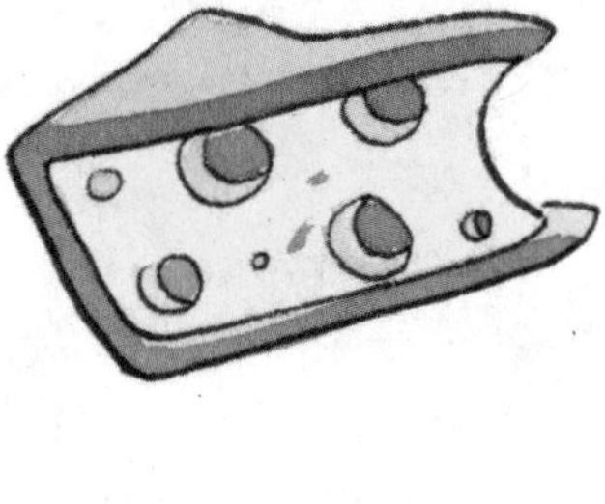

Dear mouse friends,
Thanks for reading, and farewell
till the next book.
It'll be another whisker-licking-good
adventure, and that's a promise!

Geronimo Stilton